If You're Happy and You Know It!

for Rae, Rowan,
Michelle & Alvin.
and a
special Thankyou
to Pauliina for the idea.

ISBN 0-439-82859-7

Illustrations copyright © 2003 by Jane Cabrera. All rights reserved.

Published by Scholastic Inc., 557 Broadway, New York, NY 10012, by arrangement with Holiday House, Inc.

SCHOLASTIC and associated logos are trademarks and/or registered trademarks of Scholastic Inc.

12 11 10 9 8 7 6 5 4 3 2 1   5 6 7 8 9 10/0

Printed in the U.S.A.   66

First Scholastic printing, October 2005

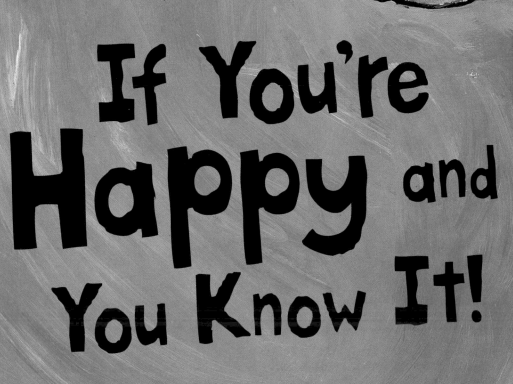

If You're Happy and You Know It!

JANE CABRERA

SCHOLASTIC INC.

New York Toronto London Auckland Sydney
Mexico City New Delhi Hong Kong Buenos Aires

Are you feeling happy today?
Join me and my friends
for some sing-along fun . . . .

If you're happy and you know it,
CLAP your hands
If you're happy and you know it,
CLAP your hands
If you're happy and you know it,
And you really want to show it

If you're happy and you know it,
CLAP YOUR HANDS!

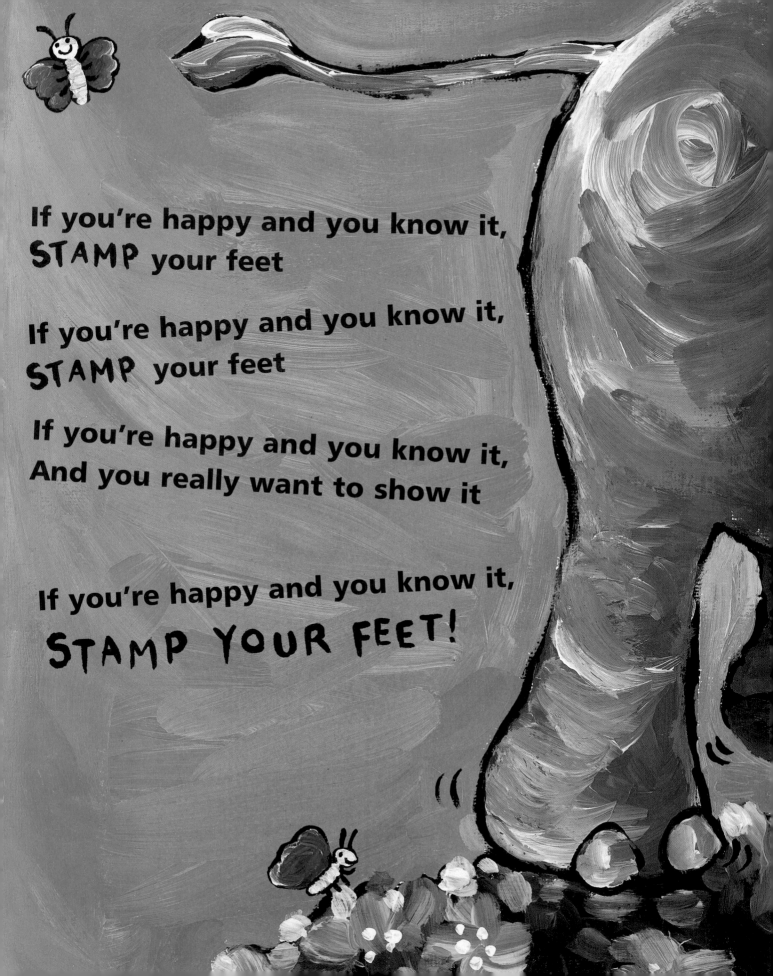

If you're happy and you know it,
STAMP your feet

If you're happy and you know it,
STAMP your feet

If you're happy and you know it,
And you really want to show it

If you're happy and you know it,
STAMP YOUR FEET!

If you're happy and you know it,
NOD your head
If you're happy and you know it,
NOD your head
If you're happy and you know it,
And you really want to show it

If you're happy and you know it,
NOD YOUR HEAD!

If you're happy and you know it,
  ROAR out loud
If you're happy and you know it,
  ROAR out loud
If you're happy and you know it,
And you really want to show it

If you're happy and
you know it,
ROAR
OUT LOUD!

If you're happy and you know it,
SPIN AROUND
If you're happy and you know it,
SPIN AROUND
If you're happy and you know it,
And you really want to show it,

If you're happy
and you know it,
SPIN AROUND!

If you're happy and you know it, FLAP your arms
If you're happy and you know it, FLAP your arms
If you're happy and you know it,

If you're happy and you know it,
   say SQUEAK SQUEAK
If you're happy and you know it,
   say SQUEAK SQUEAK
If you're happy and you know it,
And you really want to show it

If you're happy and you know it, say SQUEAK SQUEAK!

If you're happy and you know it, JUMP AROUND!
If you're happy and you know it, JUMP AROUND!
If you're happy and you know it,
And you really want to show it
If you're happy and you know it,
JUMP AROUND!

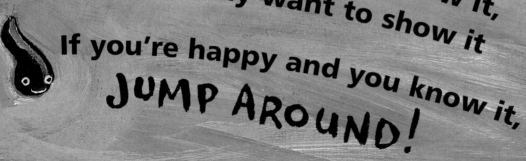

If you're happy and you know it . . .

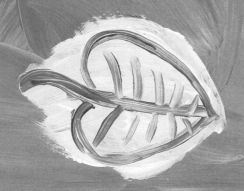

STAMP YOUR FEET!

NOD YOUR HEAD!

GO KISS KISS!

FLAP YOUR ARMS!

**If you're happy and you know it,
And you really want to show it
If you're happy and you know it,**

SHOUT...